That Kind of Danger

D0088434

Barnard New Women Poets Series
Edited by Christopher Baswell and Celeste Schenck

1986   *Heredity*
Patricia Storace
With an Introduction by Louise Bernikow

1987   *Laughing at Gravity: Conversations with Isaac Newton*
Elizabeth Socolow
With an Introduction by Marie Ponsot

1988   *The World, the Flesh, and Angels*
Mary B. Campbell
With an Introduction by Carolyn Forche

1989   *Channel*
Barbara Jordan
With an Introduction by Molly Peacock

1990   *All of the Above*
Dorothy Barresi
With an Introduction by Olga Broumas

1991   *The Stenographer's Breakfast*
Frances McCue
With an Introduction by Colleen J. McElroy

1992   *We Are the Young Magicians*
Ruth Forman
With an Introduction by Cherríe Moraga

Donna Masini

That
Kind of Danger

With an Introduction by Mona Van Duyn

Beacon Press / Boston

Beacon Press
25 Beacon Street
Boston, Massachusetts 02108-2892

Beacon Press books
are published under the auspices of
the Unitarian Universalist Association of Congregations.

Excerpt from "Walking Around" by Pablo Neruda, from *Residencia en la Tierra*,
© 1933, reprinted by permission of Agencia Literaria Carmen Balcells; English
translation by Donna Masini.

99 98 97 96 95   8 7 6 5 4 3 2

The Barnard New Women Poets Series
is supported in part by funds given
in memory of Barbara and Marilyn Meyers.

Text design by Lisa Diercks

Library of Congress Cataloging-in-Publication Data

Masini, Donna.
    That kind of danger / Donna Masini;
    with an introduction by Mona Van Duyn.
        p.   cm. — (Barnard new women poets series)
    ISBN 0-8070-6822-5 (cl). —ISBN 0-8070-6823-3 (pa)
    I. Title.   II. Series.
PS3563.A78551994
811'.54—dc20   93-36956

In Memory of

Audre Lorde

and

James Wright

for

Judd Tully

Contents

Acknowledgments

Grateful acknowledgment is made to the editors and publishers of
the following books and journals in which these poems, or
versions of these poems, have appeared:

Boulevard: "Diorama"
Georgia Review: "Hunger"
High Plains Literary Review: "Claim"; "Giants in the Earth"
Madison Review: "Home"; "My Mother Makes Me a Geisha Girl";
    "Nightscape"
New Letters: "For My Husband Sleeping Alone"
Paris Review: "At the Bandshell by the River"
Parnassus: "Today for the First Time I Listen"; "Looks That Kill"
Pequod: "Moving In and Moving Up"; "Beauty"; "At the Exhibit
    of Peter Hujar's Photographs, Grey Art Gallery, NYC, 1990"
Southern Poetry Review: "Nights My Father"
Yellow Silk: Journal of the Erotic Arts: "Learning to Swim"; "Girl,
    Gingerpot, Tree"; "Familiar"

Many thanks to the Corporation of Yaddo, the New York
Foundation for the Arts, and the National Endowment for the
Arts for support and assistance crucial to the forming of this book.

I would like to extend my deepest thanks to Jan Heller Levi,
Dorothy Barresi, Carol Conroy, Rita Gabis, Martha Gallahue, June
Jordan, Helen Lee, Regina McBride, and my parents. Thanks also
to Mona Van Duyn, Chris Baswell, and Celeste Schenck.

Introduction

Let's not hear any more wailing about contemporary American poetry's having "withdrawn from the mainstream of life," become "academic," become "solipsistic," no longer able to speak of real things to the willing reader! Let's instead start reading women's poetry and find out what nonsense these charges are. Let's, in fact, get off to a flying start with Donna Masini's book, *That Kind of Danger*.

The poems are, among other things, about America, the America of the city, each one brimming, spilling over, with its people, its felt life—a life lived and brilliantly shared with us through the open, honest, warm, unfaltering eyes, feelings, and thoughts of a remarkable woman. Walking the streets at night when the city tears itself down and rebuilds itself, as, she feels, the body's "bone, tissue, and skin, the cells . . . pumping digestions,/ the networks of neuron, dendrite, the bustle of the dream pulse" also are torn down and rebuilt at night, we see with her "the empty lot at the edge of Brooklyn, cracked glass and gravel,/ bent cans, tampon wrappers, the overpass, the echo beneath,/ . . . the projects sulking in the distance."

> As some knew tree, fish, bird, the patterns and habits,
> I knew brick and concrete, glass and light,
> the diamond sidewalks that burned in the summers,
> round-stoned walkways that shone in the rain,
> the cement walk, boxed squares for handball, slate blocks
>   thrust up by the movement of trees.

And, as the poet more and more closely embraces, merges with, the streets, hoping that "something could be made of all this breaking," imagery subtly enters and illuminates the merger of self and city.

> A shovel falls against the truck's flank.
> Below the streetlife, above the subway systems, the iron
> > girders brace,
> and still the machinery plunges, breaking ground, turning the
> > dirt, tenderly, as you'd lift a lover's buttock;
> steel pipes like metal pelvises scattered across the pavement,
> the banging of tools falling in a strange blue light.

The long rhythmic cast of the line, baited with metaphors so fresh and natural that we are for an instant almost fooled into mistaking art for speech ("I laugh—at nothing—the way a baby laughs at wallpaper"), brings in a rich catch of insight, story, past, present, picture, people—in a word, life. A bridge goes up, bringing more "greenhorns" from one settlement to another ("Pierced ears, vegetable smells. / Dense mobs mooing and shoving off the Staten Island Ferry"), where before there was only one other Italian family who owned the grocery store:

> Sarah Dominica who everyone said had spiders
> in that teased black hair. *A rat's nest*
> so high it knocked the cake display sign over the register.

The dying immigrant grandfather who used to stir the polenta arises from the poems; the grease-blackened father, "thick soot worms under his nails," who went down into mysterious depths to repair furnaces, boilers; the mother who is "everywhere," whose adult sexuality enabled her to costume and make up her daughter as a geisha girl, frightening the unready child; the Chinese waiter who peed in the lot; the squatters who slowly worked their way up the stairs into her very being—people glimpsed, watched, loved, feared, lived-with. I want to compare

Masini with Whitman, but Whitman comes off so badly beside her. He boasts, he asserts: "I am large, I contain multitudes," but we must take him on faith. By the time this poet, learning to swim, arrives at her question, "How can I float with the weight of these lives inside me?" we have *seen* those living, breathing bodies standing before us in the wide hug of her poems. She has added them to us.

Her masterpiece, if one had to choose, may be "Looks That Kill," the comingling of adolescence (with its strange, brutal surges of unmodulated sexuality) and war (with its violence, napalm, *its* burning flesh); the pity for and fear of both in an inextricable tangle:

> I am murderous and kindly.
> . . . .
> I didn't know yet you have to learn how to live,
> to distinguish between hells: a burned village, a broken date.
> I wanted to be beautiful.

As in some of the other poems the guilt, pain, and excitement of experience fall over the edge of what one thought a poem could contain, could bear.

I challenge anyone who has read through this book's passionate and successful struggle to show, tell, and find meaning movingly, to reach the last passage of the last poem without a moistening of the eye or quiver of the breath. Searching for constellations in the dark sky, "Random, irrational / as love, no matter what pictures we pretend to find," she mourns, "Oh how I have wanted things to be clear," but feels for a long time as she looks into space—"into the flicker / of history, already dead to somewhere else"—that "Patternless as measles the stars are." If anyone arrives at the tentative, hard-won end unmoved, I urge that stony reader never to open another book of poems.

I have spent a couple of weeks reading and re-reading the Barnard finalists' first-book manuscripts, written by women from all parts of the country. I think we must let the young women poets show us the complexities of our troubled, vital, sleazy, lyrical, almost indescribably diverse country for a while. Free finally to drape themselves in decorum or to burn it like a flag, unafraid of feeling and unafraid of its expression, artful as that first and most famous of their predecessors among fallen angels, they know how to do it.

MONA VAN DUYN

No quiero seguir siendo raíz en las tinieblas,
vacilante, extendido, tiritando de sueño,
hacia abajo, en las tripas mojadas de la tierra,
absorbiendo y pensando, comiendo cada día.

No quiero para mí tantas desgracias.
No quiero continuar de raíz y de tumba,
de subterráneo solo, de bodega con muertos
ateridos, muriéndome de pena.

PABLO NERUDA
"Walking Around"

(I don't want to go on being a root in the dark,
wavering, stretched out, shivering with sleep,
down in the soaked guts of the earth,
absorbing and thinking, eating every day.

I don't want so many misfortunes.
I don't want to continue as root and tomb,
alone underground, in a vault with corpses
grown stiff with cold, dying of pain.)

I.

Giants in the Earth

I walk at night, the city building and breaking around me,
over cracked concrete, over broken pavement, over steel plates
the ground bumpy, uneven beneath me.
I listen for the joy inside my bones,
the steady, even transportation of my blood.
I go down to watch the trucks, the men climb into the earth,
the pulse and rhythm of the city slower, the cadence looser.
Soon I am among them: builders, diggers, sweating their
    nightly excavations;
sandblast, jackhammer, the city making itself over, sloughing
    off layers.
I love the way things get built at night: people, the body
    rebuilding itself,
bone, tissue, and skin, the cells of the dermis, the pumping
    digestions,
the networks of neuron, dendrite, the bustle of the dream pulse.

Caterpillar. FIAT ALIA. Dynahoe 490.
Week by week the machinery moves across Delancey Street,
closer to the river where the pulse begins, slowly,
as I imagine dinosaurs moved. Heavy legs over mud and
    vegetation.

The forklift moves forward, lifts, as a priest raises a chalice.
Dynahoe 490 swivels to face it.
A man leans in his seat, grips the wheel, grasps the shift,
lifts the claw to raise the long arm,
claws a clump of rocky concrete to the street below,

3

the teams of men still digging around him. He
lifts shifts dumps, lifts shifts dumps,
the torchlights of the welders sparking in the dug-out hole
against the black night, bridge lights, four bent men circle
a trashcan fire, warming themselves, whisking their hands back
    from the sparks.
And the sparks flying out of the ground look like hell
    splintering.

Now it seems they are breaking the city down:
streets, trees, buildings coming down; broken lives, lines to
    families broken;
breaking down buildings and grandfathers, bridges, traditions,
the uprooted on their corners.
Thirty-two-year-old men in their beds.

Dreams are the places roots rock.
It comes to me now, one of those nonplaces the mind keeps
returning to: the empty lot at the edge of Brooklyn, cracked
    glass and gravel,
bent cans, tampon wrappers, the overpass, the echo beneath,
and no one to hear it except the screaming child, the projects
    sulking in the distance.

As some knew tree, fish, bird, the patterns and habits,
I knew brick and concrete, glass and light,
the diamond sidewalks that burned in the summers,
round-stoned walkways that shone in the rain,
the cement walk, boxed squares for handball, slate blocks thrust
    up by the movement of trees.

The vibration of jackhammers thrills me, shatters me.
That something could be made of all this breaking.
Sweet rain and sweat and the lovely yellow machinery
    knocking,
the black gravel curved as the shell of a turtle.

I stand a long time watching them, lean across the fissure into a
    wood-slat hole.
A man's red eyes glow up at me. He grins, unhooks the lamp
    from his belt and climbs out of the ground.

Sometimes it feels like it's me breaking apart.

What is the name of that truck, that tool?
What are you making? Where are your children?
What is the sound of a body breaking, the cells rebuilding, the
    heart deteriorating?

The forklift turns.
A shovel falls against the truck's flank.
Below the streetlife, above the subway systems, the iron girders
    brace,
and still the machinery plunges, breaking ground, turning the
    dirt, tenderly, as you'd lift a lover's buttock;
steel pipes like metal pelvises scattered across the pavement,
the banging of tools falling in a strange blue light.

Woman to Woman

How loud your heart sounded
pounding above me, around me
confusing the mineral and liquid that nourished me
as I coiled and built inside you
my cells dividing away from you
shyly bearing their identical messages
intimate, familiar
dazzle of synaptic spasms,
a milky protein forming the arched spine,
the ear, the lip, the pod of the egg sacs.
How I clenched inside your muscle and bone.

Under your insistent heart
I rocked and coiled,
learned my gravitation to choked places.
That dull beat tracked me,
an underthump scudding behind me, within me
confusing itself with my own.
It cleaved to me, clung to me, hung
through the contours of childhood,
dogged me through schoolyard and grotto,
the lavatory static where white tiles whizzed
with the groan of your humming.

I wear your skin, your hair, your eyes,
push away from a man I love waiting for one who will
fit to me, cleave to me, know what I mean
as I whisper *green, cold, pine-tar, I am hungry.*

Did I fracture you as I broke through?
Did I leave you split, torn,
one half bending to silence
the violence of your other stalking me,
waving a fist of my hair?

I thought I could build my life
out of hard things and soft things
out of wind-swept dust of city air, coffee,
and hair-fringed dill, stripped oak, the ecology of skin.
You are everywhere.

I walk. I rock. I jaw through the nights
as if I could chew my way out of you.
I walk. I rock: thorax, lumbar, sacrum,
the long horn of me curved
searching my own sounds, clenched and grizzly.
The gnash and crackle awakens a woman beside me—
lusty, pulsing, curled in her own long dream of renewal.
Her body makes itself over as she sleeps,
as she stretches first one leg, then another,
easing the burden of her torso,
releasing what she has held within her
through the night.

Nights My Father

We never knew exactly what our father did
in dark basements, late into the night.
His work clothes, cellar smells.
The dark came out of him.
Dirt green, creased black,
ACE in big red letters
a yellow diamond stitched across his back,
below the earth with rats and tar,
roaches, spiders, waterbugs.
Only he knew the way out.

Underground by the oilburners
where the heat went dead
he crawled into iron mouths
hauled out fists of oily sludge.
Could a man get trapped in there?
Scars, creases where grease seeped in, never came out,
thick soot worms under his nails,
he rolled the hose from tanks to valves
ladies, alligators curled in basements.
When the harbor froze he slept on the floor by his truck.

In the middle of the night there was something
in our kitchen,
rattling through the silverware
in our kitchen drawer.
In the gold night light, a bear,

the thick fur breathing.
I aimed a gun. I shot.
The fur parted.
It was my father. His good suit pressed
but the hands stuck out: greasy hands,
so black the creases darkened as he washed them.

He didn't need anyone. He could do it alone.
Boilers humming, clanging, air banging, heat building.
There she goes, he'd yell,
at the center of the earth,
where the heat is, and rough hands,
men's hands. The way they touch.
Warm men with rough hands
cha-cha bossa nova
the snoring comes from that place,
low sounds the body makes.

Our father heated people in winter,
and he danced our mother
with the grace of a bear,
under red bulbs,
by the Christmas tree
the pudding black, so black,
a cake of shaking oil.

I remember him in winter
mornings when I wake,
the bridge hanging across the street in the snow
trucks skidding, whispering in the icy sun.
The whispers from the bedroom,

the creaking of the floor, the whispers,
the dark something dropping,
then he snorted through the night
water dripped, radiators popped.

Don't touch him, we screamed,
as he came through the door,
my head in his work clothes.
The dark coming out.
All night the glazy stare at the TV set.
Heart. Get it going. He begins to stamp and steam.
He went under, down under streets, gratings,
the places men went.
Could a man get trapped in there?
Graves. Caves. Boilers. Crawling.
Nights I heard him humming.

Home

Their inward thought is that their houses shall continue forever,
and their dwelling places to all generations.

Psalm 49:11

Today in this wet place
where hedges lean and sway in the rain,
trees bend, creak, spring back,
at the time of month when water builds in me,
waits its release,
I make a place for myself
to face the despair of my parents.
No whispered the thin plaster
walls of our house,
the doors that warped and would not lock.
Sin hissed through the humid rooms:
the living room, gravid, mud-colored, my mother's room,
through the kitchen where my father's bathrobe
ignited
with the ash and flame of his forgotten pipe,
where we put that fire out;
where my eight-year-old brother took the knife
from my hands, rocked me
as our breath condensed on the windows,
salted the air,
rained.
It is said oceans build in this way.

Water collected in that house.
My father could not look at me.

It became dense with us
the wallpaper peeled, hung in long damp strips,
the basement flooded
the backyard sunk under the weight of rain.
Storms, floods,
the weather of childhood,
even the ceilings bloated and dripped
as though the house wept and sweated with us.
There was a bone-chill in the beams
an awful creaky leaning that caused
the walls to sag, the molding to lift and warp.

Outside the weeping willow leaned
into the upstairs bedroom window,
rotted water sucked out of the swamp—
that kind of danger.
Its brown leaves hung with disease dropped
sticky black worms that stuck to our shoes.
City people, we didn't understand
what would happen once our tree was gone.
All day that awful buzzing then the sun
shone over the stump into the panes
and now we wouldn't have to fear the tree
would fall. A hundred years at least
and we knocked it down one afternoon.

My father could not absorb that water.
It rolled off him, left grease streaking his thick trunk.
My mother took it into her bones. She wheezed
and hung through steam for years
waiting to heal. When pneumonia entered
she took the house down with her.

The backyard grass grew so wild
we had to hack it with scythes
in high boots, stomping through breeding mosquitoes.
A heavy cloud hung over us.
We had tampered with something.

What Drives Her

She knows how dangerous it is
to yield, here on the dance floor.
Music so loud she can see it
creating waves, striations in the air,
lights, bodies, pulsing, desire
enticing as the smell of sex.
Its various shapes enter her, lead her.

Invisible filaments begin to connect her
to the bodies of strangers, to the floor.
She leans into the music, into light,
men, women, necks, chests, eyes,
a collision of hips. She could slip
into their skin, their sweat.
It is like swimming.

She has come to this place ready to spill,
as though she'd been carrying herself,
carefully, for days, trying not to tip.
As though night were a container
and she a leaking thing.
She thinks everyone can see this.
Across the floor a mirror in which
she does not recognize herself.

She takes in the man leaning toward her,
the light in his hair.
She could walk in that hair,

fly in it, nameless, brainless.
She takes in his eyes. He is watching
yes, moving toward her, back,
bent at the hip, she provokes,
he withdraws, listing, teasing.
This is better than fucking
most people.

What drives her is the exquisite
moment when you can't tell yourself
from the body opposite.
Better than touching
the promise of touch.
All night it rolls,
muscular, undulant, the pressing
roomful of strangers wanting
to become one moving, breathing being.

Hours collide.
I becomes she.
She knows if she can
get to the,
just to the,
just to the, oh
she is everyone, leans into whatever
is close: those eyes, the beat, this night.
It is what she imagines heaven to be—
a little confusing
music threading through her,
each hair standing, reaching
bodies moving, shaking, watching,
the floor beneath her inside, outside,

seeping up into her body.
She cannot imagine stopping.
Someone, she thinks,
will have to stop me.

What spills out, the part
of her that cannot keep her own secrets,
that gives it all away.
What evaporates: telephones, notebooks,
love and the names of things.
Won't someone please stop her?

Later that night the room still spins in her.
She cannot sleep.
Her father dances inside her,
a kind of dim, gritty music.
And her heart, her insistent heart,
floats up panting
as though shaken up
from a buried place.

Familiar

As I pick up your pants,
fold them over the chair
I remember the time I fell
off a barstool into your lap,
the first time my hands traveled
the curved distance of your shirt
across the belt's boundary
along the ridges of your hips.
How the back seam split you into two hemispheres
I dug my hands in earth
and coming around your thighs
approached your sex in its curled dream of adventure.
We raced out, ran along Houston Street
crossed the Bowery to your front
door and up the stairs.
I remember you dove into me, wild and eager,
how we knocked and turned on your wood floor
this before I knew
the way you drink your morning coffee
read before you fall asleep
before I knew you would dive and dive
and I would come to know the angle of your hipbone
like the contour of my knee
before I knew that someday
I'd climb into bed and find you
sleeping over my copy of Kafka's *Metamorphosis*,

that I would take off your glasses
pull the book from your hands
turn off the light
and lie a long time
listening to you sleep.

Looks That Kill

I dream of a burning village and I dream I can save it,
lay the cool weight of my body across it, a balm.
Fatigued, I go searching.

War erupts all over the city:
movies, posters, one-man shows,
rootless vets, refugees weave,
stumble through subway cars, cardboard homes.
It begins to grow again inside me,
this living through it twice.

In 1967 I began to leak blood. Eggs dropped
Hanoi, Dak To, Khe Sanh
somewhere a village burned
somewhere a people destroyed
and the eggs kept dropping.
I wrapped my shame in the pages of the Staten Island Advance
I didn't know yet you have to learn how to live,
to distinguish between hells: a burned village, a broken date.
I wanted to be beautiful.

I hold a mirror to my crotch
slit, gash, cunt, snatch
fractured as the earth cracks with a steady plate grind.
A blond boy kisses my face, loses himself
in a tangle of hair, the age-old push and thrust.
The hymen tears, blood spots the basement floor.
Rituals of love, jerking courtships

writing and twisting on the dance floor
In-A-Gadda-Da-Vida pounding through high school gyms
flying over rice fields.

All across America
napalmed breasts and children smolder in a burning glue.
All across America
bowling dinners and shiny cars.
We learn to live in a torn place.

These gooks have no respect for life, her father says as she slashes
    her arms in the bathroom.

I am splitting apart—
in movie theaters, in libraries under dull fluorescent,
in supermarkets before a glass case my face disintegrates.
I have felt a child toss and press, end up a few days' blood.
A failure of nerve.
I have rubbed against a mirror as though I could be both sides
    of the sex act.
I have read of beatings and burials and wished for a more
    beautiful face.
I have felt the ache of sex and the revulsion of sex in the same
    bed.
I have woken with a swollen cock shoved down my throat
and dreamed of beating a pregnant woman.
I have accepted a man dissolving inside me and admired the
    bravery,
the daring of him to shoot it into me.
I have given up what I want to get what I need—
merging, urgent, craving.
I have offered myself as a boat, a bridge.

I have taken love and twisted it; wrung it, hung it in the
    window.
I have wanted to be heroic.

A man lies across me. I no longer see his face
etched across my skull.
I could make him anything.
I am murderous and kindly.
I have rolled and pummeled across this floor until I don't know
    between the soreness of my body
and the soreness of my heart.
I could destroy you, I tell him.

I have wanted to be heroic, to bring back the dead.
I have heard the low growl inside and watched it burst into
    tigers.
They are the color of napalm.
Leaping in the quiet streets.
I think I should be behind bars.

The spine splinters, splits my body to zones:
stomach, bladder, spleen. Places no one has touched.
The fist of my heart beats against bone chips,
opens to headlines, photographs:
    Mariner's Harbor Boy, 19, Dead
    Great Kills Marine, 21, Gunned Down
    New Dorp Sgt., 21, Dead in Vietnam
    Tottenville Graduate, Felled by Mine
I clip out the faces, take them down to Great Kills Beach
as though I could heal them,
as though they might re-enter the world.
Teach me to live, I pray.

My heart closes around them. I sew armbands, peace signs,
call them killer.

The muddy voice hauled from slime dragging the roots and
      violences of families,
the thin, reedy voice, a palm of despair.
She goes digging to find what she has buried:
the mother grinning with a fist of her hair
the naked Jesus beaten and pierced
the knife in the bathroom
the pelvis bashed under a kitchen clock.
She wakes with a cock purpling in her mouth, a torpedo.
She goes searching for its owner among the slumped and
      moaning.
She tugs and pulls and cannot remove it
the peristalsis of her body pumping to dislodge it.
She carries it with her, a purple, swollen thing
as a snake throats a rabbit, hours of digestive work.
Such is an adolescence fattened on war,
the Asian battleground, the kitchen table
the rumble of echo and answer
words not her own and words her own knocking against one
      another.
Whose cock is this anyway?

I dream of a burning village and I dream I can save it.

Concerts, assassinations, search and destroy.
Eggs drop. The helicopter of memory obliterates.
Fragments of words, lives splitting, exploding.
The sentence disintegrates.
Language. Desire. I have no more stories.

These days when he enters I admire the bravery,
the way he surrenders,
the white flag of his love burning.
Lie down in peace.
He makes up my body, reconstitutes the parts.
I could destroy him. It would be that easy.
Hold me. Hold me together.
Fragments of nightmares and fingers
putting together a life out of phrases.
And the general's words:
We had to destroy it to save it.

Is it possible to enter another's life?
Is it possible to heal it?
How can I reconcile the violence of dreams with the tenderness
    of hair?
Each person I touch shatters in my hands.
The seductive eyes of a stranger look me over, the danger
    escapes him.
I have walked down quiet streets
a cock lodged in my throat.
Help me. Unhook me.
Take the parts and piece them together.
I no longer understand the logic of sentences.
Fragments. Shrapnel.
Make love. Wage war.
Lick my body clean.
Take the smear of blood from my teeth.
Make them gleam.

Eye of the Skull

After the needle I lie back. The dentist waits
while the novocaine takes—then starts to work. He pokes,
prods, presses the drill into my tooth. I hear the roots
move. I feel—pressure—but nothing
more. The nerve is dead for now and I wonder
where does pain go. My body is taking
in this pain and it is going somewhere,
someplace, and I am not feeling
this or anything except maybe sleepy. I am sleepy
in his wide-armed chair, falling out or falling
off remembering

when I fell off a horse. Not a real horse, a rocking
horse. I slid down the hard, smooth, plastic flank,
in one sweet flash of glee I flew,
or thought I flew, face flat to the ground.
There was blood, blue swollen gums, my teeth
knocked back and up but what I remember most
is that my uncle gave me a dollar,
that I sipped soup through a straw, only I only
remember the first night which makes me think,
since it took months and months to heal,
that we can get used to anything. Anything

will, in time, seem normal: a spectacular view, loss
of sight, legs, even people though still there are certain
streets, turns of phrase, faces—memory's flash—
suspended, illuminated, rosy. I don't know why

I only remember moments. Why shouldn't I, with my good
memory remember everything? Every day, every breakfast.
Did my mother throw the soft-cooked egg at me every
    morning? It seems
to me she did, that every day I bashed my head into a wall
and maybe it was only once, or several times, a dream
at the base bowl of the toilet,
it was white, white . . .

Where does pain go, I wonder
walking downtown from the dentist's office,
my mouth numb, tongue thick,
lips like they're a part
of someone else's face. I hear
behind me the harsh voice of a woman. An older woman
dressed as a young girl. She had gone to a good school,
liked good things. Had had them too. You could tell.
She is screaming into herself, into the air. Vulgar things,
shouting them to no one in particular
that I can see.

What is trapped in the bones, the gearlike teeth
that join the two fused cramped parts
of the skull? What clenches and curls in the marrow?
Did the pain surface, just then? Did all that
numbed pain come in one great rush?
Does all the pain and all the hurt you felt and did not feel
burst out in one bald scream that one day, catches you,
companions you down a street. Do you talk to that pain,
scream to it, with it, from it, as if it were
a friend, a very old acquaintance,
your destination all along?

At the Bandshell by the River

This place, too, has its own integrity:
split, ruined, abandoned
walls of chipped blue cursed
with black names, red dates, green rage
it stands here quiet in the cool salt taste of the morning.
Today the iron gates are open—
no need to belly under the rusted bars
pressing myself into dirt and weed
after a night of a thousand mirrors, taunting, humorless,
my mother in my hipbones shrieking, father my knees,
tomorrows of a grandfather who sailed out of humped Italian
    caves,
coarse inland dreams
to a country where he fathered twelve children and died
far from the streets he called home.

How have I used his rough, stocky hands?
Where have I carried the few loose strands of his hair?
The fig trees he planted still ripen within me.

This morning I am loose as a river.
I laugh—at nothing—the way a baby laughs at wallpaper.
I follow the run of squirrels down curved wood benches in
    descending arcs
through the open theater once filled
with music, crowds, lovers sharing fruits from net bags,
restless children pressing bubble gum under bench slats,
performers stretching, sweating in the wings;

and the plane trees, the oaks, maples, lindens
the sap smell of their sex sticky.
The sun tongues its way out of the morning fog.
Through the gash at the back of the bandshell
the glint and twist of the river draws me forward,
up the cracked stairs across the bare proscenium.

Backstage the sun cuts through crumbling walls, falls
through the open ceiling, over collapsed
rafters and fallen staircases, falls
on brick and rubble, broken track lights, cigarette packs,
pill bottles, wine bottles, old needles, a rusted washtub.
A nervous music fills the space: birdcall, squirrel-run,
mosquito, fly, pigeon, rat, sparrow,
the quick, particular movements whizzing over beams,
    whistling, calling.
I stand and listen at the brink of myself,
certain only of this, of this,
and the steady lisp of the river lapping.

II.

Who Giveth This Woman

You married me, now you're stuck
digging, hauling, clogged
in the walls of me.
I am ooze, silt,
I am the daughter of a man who dug grease
out of the mouths of broken boilers
out of holes that didn't heat
the daughter of a man who heated houses
burning in his American oil.
The first time I saw the whites of his eyes
through the grease in his face
I knew I'd never love another man
who blackened in basements days, nights
turning darker as the years went. Soot of the caves.
A migration of sweat.
I'd go for the clean sort: elegant, angular,
hard and smooth as a carved bone soul-catcher
held to the mouth to heal, to trap
all these strange voices shrieking and knocking inside me,
the woman rising out of the mud
reaching for me. Lips for my lips.
Stay, she says, you are one of us.
Each night you sink into me I can feel
the greased heat, underground boiling
rumblings in the tunnels of me.
Go ahead. Dig in. I'm watching you.
Sometimes I can't even feel
the rats crawling inside me

the fist digging, knuckling. Go ahead
fuck the mother out of me.
Did you know it would be such a filthy job
you there heaving and sweating above me?
I'm so far away I can barely see you
now you're dark as I am.

Hunger

Deprived of a kind of salt I grew
to an insatiable craving.
I tried to eat rocks. I snapped
shut on a terrible hunger.
I hid from my mother—her black bras,
her spike heels, her curses and weeping.
I watched her. I dreamed her dead.
Her voice became the noise of my body.
I followed the blue veins on the backs
of her thighs as she leaned out the window
reeling in the clothes. I was taken
by her stories: the yellow pellets
she kneaded into margarine sacks,
a young girl, working it.
How it moved in her hands
deepening, undulant. Hunger I tasted
in the breeze she left behind. I hid from her
in closets that smelled of failure
and wings that ate holes in our clothes.
Where she kept the dead fox she snapped
about her throat. Teeth biting tail.
Coarse fur. Beady eye. I hid
from her teased hair and her lipsticks,
her shadows and powders and tears.
If I am not careful I leak black hands,
my father's desire falls from my mouth
a frail and ashy carbon, a black crease
forms in the folds of my arms. I follow

strange men, a whistle in my hands,
green about my eyes, bending into the night.
There is not enough night for me.
I want to roll through the roots of ancient oaks,
lick salt from the necks of people I love
wake every morning to a human smell,
sex in my clothes, something warm
and salty in my mouth.

That White Sustenance

We drank her sadness.
Grew fat on it.
Despair. A soft word.
Whispered. Milky. Silken.
Swollen. Even the angel
on the Christmas tree tipped
forward into the circle of torpor
into white pools waiting
for each child to dip, fill up,
until one by one
she placed us rocking on a shelf
under the ticking clock
by the moon through gauzy curtains.

Before the Bridge: A Story

I.

"Too bad they didn't know the house was built on swamp,"
Joe Reese laughed to Grace Vance one Sunday after the rain,
my parents in the backyard bailing out the basement,
us kids feet-up on a pile of rocks.

The house leaned. The mud-sod oozed.

Stupid guineas.
These people from Brooklyn.
Greenhorns my mother called the ones just over.
Pierced ears, vegetable smells.
Dense mobs mooing and shoving off the Staten Island ferry.

We came over before the bridge went up,
no other Italians
except the Dominicas who owned the grocery.
Sarah Dominica who everyone said had spiders
in that teased black hair. *A rat's nest*
so high it knocked the cake display sign over the register.
I wondered if it came off at night, the spiders
and what else tangled in her hair.
I dreamed of Sarah Dominica's hair, breeding
spiders at the roots; her brother Joe who lost
his arm leaning out a bus,
wore a long-sleeved shirt knotted at the wrist,

packed sandwiches with his good right arm.
"Italians," Grace said, "and more coming over with the bridge
    going up."

2.

The bridge was going up—the Verazzano-Narrows—
the longest, highest, suspension
bridge in the world,
and Thomas Fleming's father worked on it.
Not at the top, where the Indians worked,
the one who slipped, fell to the harbor.
"Indians love heights," my father said.
"They're made to work on bridges."
I thought of him falling, drowning,
how they said he must have died before he hit.
I wondered if Indians loved water too,
what made them want to work up high.
"Staten Island must be wild," I said,
"if there's still Indians here."
"They're different now," my mother said.
"No more feathers and beads."

3.

When the builders came to Great Kills, rats ran down Hylan
    Boulevard.
I slogged through mud with Carol Keane, Gus Eklund, and my
    . brother Gregg,
hunting for arrowheads, back in the woods
where new developments were going up.

All I ever found were pointy rocks.
We slogged and climbed and filled our pockets,
then one by one
jumped from the peaks of the high dirt piles.
"Geronimo," Carol yelled and jumped.
"Geronimo," Gus yelled and jumped.
"Geronimo," I yelled and stood, too scared to jump until my
    brother shoved me and I fell,
belly-whopping the swampy mud.
"Look out for rats," Gus yelled.
"Crawl like a pig," Carol yelled.
"A guinea pig! A guinea pig!" my brother screamed, leaping
down, pounding his mouth, whooping around and
around me rooting in the mud.

Nightscape

It's not only my lights that hum in this city
through the arc of night
at two a.m. when I'm up again, waiting.
There's the lights of the bridge, a disinterested moon,
blue TV glare by the carwash downstairs where
three black men blink into forty-year-old love scenes
and rock in their chairs.
A purple light hangs soft by the river.
In a bright yellow light a mother suckles her child
her head falling over its hungry mouth.
Upstairs a man knocks his wife to the floor,
drunk again, no light in her
but the heat of their angers spark and fall
to the windows below.
Under nodding streetlights junkies trade shoot waste,
the Chinese waiter pees in the lot,
the taxi driver lights a cigarette, waits for his fare,
the policeman slams his car door, runs for a beer.
Who is the fireman who masturbates urgently as his wife sleeps
       beside him dreaming of fire,
who curls in his sleep unwilling to wake,
who types unfamiliar names and addresses on envelopes
       calculating
the chickens and shoes she will buy with the extra cash,
who scrawls in her notebook the dream of a woman to hold
       her,
who holds her new lover imagining his history of fucking,
who fondles his pistol reliving the mother who beat him?

Lovers, destroyers, move through this city through so many
  windows
it seems no one is sleeping.
Vigilant, restless, I chew the cords of my own unraveling
  hungers,
split into a roomful of pictures that shimmer along walls.
I join the ring of rootless insomniacs, trying to chisel a shape
  out of longing,
to say, yes, here is a white bowl on the windowsill, and beyond
  that
the street-echo, and men who sleep under mattress-tents by the
  river
as though night itself were a big house.

Sleep and Marriage

I touch him with my hands, with their constant
smell of cigarettes, stroke
his winged hip that slowly lifts with his breathing.
I touch him with grief that sees in the dark
and refuses to sleep.
I touch him with the odor of longing.
I touch him with my voice, with its buried
melodies of a twelfth-century nun,
the light she sang, the white glass, the asters.
I touch his bones.
I believe the bones in the museum once walked across
       Manhattan.
With hands of cigarettes and death, I touch him.
With love, its war paint and horses, I touch him.
He is dreaming. I see it in his lips.

I have disappointed him with my Sundays, my night walks,
my cornered smile. I love him
in moments, by the ocean where he skims stones,
years falling from him, from us. We ran
through the dunes to the ocean forgetting
the way people leave us, the way dunes
shift, sand displacing rock, drifting steeper.
The digital lights flicker and switch, minutes tick.
Time moves with the slow steady steps
night takes to walk into morning.
He is not mine now. He belongs to regions

where monkeys ride buses and frogs kiss the hem of a young
   girl's skirt.
I understand nothing but the race of blood through my fingers:

God in the veins of my neck
God in the breath that settles inside me
God in the dirt under my nails
in the frogs and buses and stones,
the urine of a red-haired boy, gold piss
the bridge that hangs by my window
whose voice rises in my groin as cities disintegrate,
and mountains give way to land, buildings
rise, anchored in a bedrock of dinosaur bones.
Still as I lie the movement continues
as a child whirls and whirls then stands stiff
to listen to the dizzy spin,
and daughters leave their mothers for torches
trailing small grains—the crushed skull dust of lovers.
I touch him through time that tumbles my dead friends
until their skulls shine.
Horses move through me, muscular, black, ridden by young
   girls,
while somewhere the curious
look to the sky through giant machines
to see history flicker,
cleave, kindle, and curl
and time's long arm cuffs them
and everywhere finds change.

Easter on Staten Island

1.

I stood at the back end of the boat
watching the city fade in a fog.
Air gray, buildings gray, water gray,
gray gulls as if on invisible string dropping up
and down and up again,
on columns of air
over the wake of the ferry,
with the sense of being tugged from behind
my life fading quickly before me, who I am
succumbing to what I was.
I thought of the fogs the ferry crossed in a blur of winters
the grim horn lowing, a solitary buoy rocking its chime
mist so thick I'd imagine docking in another time.
I was always hoping disaster might strike, carry us out
of our everyday lives. Schoolyards, dentists.
Something big enough to hold us,
binding our future, as when a country is invaded,
the crowds face the tanks.

2.

Down Wiman Avenue, across the boulevard to the water
where fading bungalows bunch together like overlapping teeth
chipped and peeling, old carnival lanterns, madonnas knocking
in the breeze, the fog slowly eating the man on the rock,
the blue-lit house, the docks eerie, careless,

to their knees in water.
When it rained the streets flooded,
the ocean backed up:
skates, toys, shoes, trash, newspapers, baby bottles
floated past our buried cars, their humpbacks gleaming.
Sometimes I forgot we lived on an island, rarely went down
below the boulevard, past the Dream Lounge, Mardi Gras
to the bungalows by the water's edge
climbed through broken windows
to a torn-up couch, old coffee stinking the room
pill bottles, hypodermic needles, adventure.
It was 1965, low lights and red chiffon when Clay Cole
and his go-go girls came to the Dream Lounge.
Father Hicks reeled at the pulpit. Keep your children
away from there. Husbands, he should have said. I imagined
Joe Reese nuzzling red chiffon as the lights blinked
and blinked behind the colored paper shades.
Seedy, my mother said.
A man planted in a woman.
A spray of sperm.
A broadcast.

3.

I blinked to keep the drink out of my face,
to keep the bones hard
at the beachfront behind Carmen's Spanish Restaurant
as a married man slid his hands down my pants
knocked me against the wood fence into the dense
fog already eating half the island.
It was one of those nights you forget
mothers and consequence,

although his wife occurred to me,
herding three kids through Korvettes, picking their shoes,
their shirts, carefully, checking the prices, her hair
the color of whiskey, greasy.
I laughed, cut my hand on the green sea glass
as I fell to my knees in the sand,
his legs, the drink, and the fog coming over.

4.

The hunger of fog sinking through air
the blind acts of a lifetime.
You escaped, I whisper into my hands
as the boat pulls toward the dock.
Manhattan: three bridges blink through mist
building tips lit in a zigzag east
rows and rows of lighted windows burn through the night.
One of them mine.
The boat creaks through the tight wood docks,
gulls sound through the holiday haze,
red wine and tedium,
the blank you become, knocking it back
when even the present looks like the past.

Wheel of Fortune

for Mauro Masini (1896–1988)

My grandfather is watching Vanna White.
His loose shirt exposes the bones of his neck.
He stares from the TV to his prayerbook and back.
He is dying.
He sinks into his ninety-two years dreaming
already another place.
One turn of the wheel and he floats out,
Vanna moves forward, shimmers
like a terrible fish,
her voracious smile a revelation of teeth.
I reach out to touch him
his shoulders bird-weak, brittle.
I want to build his village around him, of air and chicken
 and pig,
the soft Tuscan earth.

I face backward to speak to him.
He is a wheel broke loose, spinning out,
his children tethered to the spokes trying to hold him.

A long time ago in a place far away . . .
so his stories begin. *We ate chestnut flour,*
raised silkworms, chickens.
I left for America with my brothers.

Brooklyn. Old home of Italians and Jews.
The streets West Indian now,
widening their legs to take in the new,
the old Granada Theater a Baha'i church.
Where are the cracks you tarred?
Young man, new beard, walking the streets of an alien city,
old man whirling through old space
grasping a wheel,
scattering prayerbook pages across Flatbush Avenue.

The gold band slips from his finger, too thin now;
the weight of its sixty-five years no longer secures him.
He's letting it all go—zippers, pajama tops, bowels, and
      grandchildren.

In a Tuscan village a garden of tombstones, photographs—
my people: MASINI carved on a churchyard wall,
terra cotta floor, floor his father laid, tile by tile.
The land he worked. The people he left.

I already miss the particular and definite
movements of his fingers
squeezing a bag of sugar and cream,
the muscular arm stirring a pot of polenta,
the cheeses, the fruits, the bowl of stewed prunes,
sign of the cross over a handful of pills.
Dante. Recipes. Ave Maria.

He is a child now,
close to beginnings.
He is younger than I am.

Ninety-two years is not long enough.

He lifts his legs, raises
his prayerbook to the TV screen,
looks up at me, blinking, expectant.
The wheel is turning

Wait, I want to whisper, say your good-byes.
Good-bye to Villa, il Volto Santo, the church on the hill,
to terra cotta, mortadella, Lucca, Firenze.
Good-bye Giovanni, Filiberto, Pietro, and Laura,
the boats that carried you to New York and the boats you
        followed going back.
Good-bye to 1910, Ellis Island, Oliver Street,
the bocci courts where you found your old tongue
the Italian Bronx where you discovered your wife,
her quick hands, her superstitions and fears.
Good-bye to Canal Street, dishwasher jobs
the German baker who taught you:
breathe life into dough—let it rise.
Good-bye to nightshifts and train rides to Brooklyn,
to Holy Cross Church, bamboo cane down Flatbush Avenue,
weak legs, unsteady hands.
Good-bye to novenas and rosaries, holy cards, candles,
to Gloria, Hugo, Bruno, Diana.
Good-bye to the oak chest.
Good-bye to the courtyards you tarred
the stone steps you painted,
the grandchildren who chipped them with stoopball and sticks.

The wheel is turning
my grandfather is sleeping.
Basta.
Dormi in pace ora.
Dante. Recipes. Ave Maria.

Winter-Seeming Summer

For months we watched my grandfather disintegrate.
He caved into his bones, a pile of old birds.
His bedroom whispered
its constant chatter of statues and beads
its centuries of saints barefoot across floorboards
remembering their noisy temptations, waiting
where medicine sleeps with prayer.
Aves flirted at the ceiling. Candle flames
collapsed down, weak into wicks
as that room drew the cold through its roots.

The windows frosted.
The mouth-ring of night called.
Grandpa, open-armed, reached for an angel
his hair white, hoarse breath
we watched him evaporate
and death began to flower on us all.

Beauty

for Steven Festa (1953–1987)

The optometrist hands me a polaroid of my eye.
I watch as the black circle fades
to a veiny planet. A fetus in its nebular sac.
The branched arteries connect to the optic
nerve where the veins cross.
He can tell a lot from the eye.
He knows what to look for—
thick lines the sign of hardening.
Mine are thin. Healthy. Beautiful, he says.

I have never thought myself beautiful,
one of the blessed who can look steady
at their own reflection, so I was surprised
when you called me beautiful.
It was summer. I was glowing.
You were almost bald. Your face
newly old. Hospital eyes, the color of waiting.
I'd brought you a mechanical dog,
wedges of melon, slivers of ginger for your throat.
I sat by your bed, by your wires and cards
and the pale green wall that could not save you,
almost obscene in my health.
You look beautiful, you said.
I laughed. I can always laugh.
I made you laugh.
I promised to visit.

I hid from your dying. It waited
for me, blew through the valves of me,
pressed itself into faces on subways,
into windows, clean towels, menus. I hid
from it as I was hidden from deaths as a child.
The floating goldfish plucked from their tanks,
flushed down toilets where they turned and surfaced
in rank dreams. You loved animals, held them—
birds, fish, lizards, dogs—as they died in your living
rooms. Sometimes I think beauty is the way you look
on as something you love fades, disintegrates,
the way you wait for the moment when the life blinks out
and what you love has slipped from its skin.
I wrote. You called. I played your voice
back. *No regrets, girl. Never*
any regrets. You're beautiful.
Your voice was blurry. I'd heard you were blind.

How much can the eye take in?
I think it must be the organ of feeling.
I could not look at you
looking at me. What a relief
to touch you, as though my hand
on your chest defined a boundary between us.
Now you were blind.
You would leave the world in pieces
and one of my eyes would begin that long turning
inward as I came to see what I'd refused.

III.

Caul

I was eleven when the world closed,
the living room choke brown
air thick as blankets.
When it was damp the plastic rhododendron
stank like a hardware store.
Sometimes I hid in the sweat-blue basement
sprawled across the old Kenmore,
the clothes clicking, spinning
in the dry heat, the metal top hot
on my stomach, and rocked.
I rocked through medicine dreams of my mother
rocked through ice wings on glass doors
rocked through oak shadows rubbing together
their trunks muscular, shuddering.
Sometimes the whole house whispered around me:
sickness, sinful.
Sometimes I slept there,
thighs gripping the bowl of light
where night swung open and the world unfolded
like the bud of a dream,
leaf green, impalpable.

Learning to See

When they discovered I needed glasses, I was already
accustomed to blur. Everything had that vague,
hazy look satin gets as it shreds.

Grass was the first thing I saw:
stiff fringe, no longer a blur of green;
dirt, glass, brick.

When the facade of a building broke down into sections
I lost a kind of wholeness.
Things began to fracture.

Edges became visible.
I missed the haze,
rainbows in puddles when the colors merged,

mothers and their children.
There was a sharpness I lacked
steady as sound.

If I squinted or lifted the corners of my eyes,
the world clicked into focus.
Glasses were different. They slid

down my nose making the world
slip. Their boundaries visible, elliptic
blue with stars at the edges.

2.

I could see best what was close.
But objects held too near broke down.
Sometimes I was eyeless as a sponge.
Possibility swirled in its misted nimbus.
I could make an autumn of a peeling wall,
ziggurats of bathroom tiles,
a dust cloud of my mother
(I could never make her wholly disappear),
her voice visible,
I can see right through you.
What could she decipher in that blurry child?
Could she see the shifting scenes I conjured,
liquid, sinful? Was I invisible?
I reflected her.
I watched my tiny self in her eye.

3.

After I was fitted for contacts
I had terrible nightmares.
The lenses throbbed,
would not fit inside.
The flimsy disk congealed in my throat,
gagged me
as I sucked to keep it wet.
At first I tried not to notice.
They made everything too clear.
I was suspicious
of this crisp and seamy vision.
People looked smaller,

everything looked smaller,
separate, lonely as a cut-out doll
without the furry edges connecting
everything to everything else.

4.

I forget to concentrate, see nothing.
My eyelids flip back, focus

old houses, old streets,
a small girl, a small room, a space cleared.

Everything was a blur, she carried it with her,
her mother's voice, a plasma surrounding her

the empty space, a ghostly weather
the way curtains look in photographs,

snow dances in glass bulbs,
the world behind it. Buried.

And families shake inside their boxes.
The projector runs. Film makes the life move.

5.

I walk these streets day after day, though I cannot resurrect
a life of those years. I ache,

succumb, as though my blood
were drained, replaced with sand.

No, the teacher says,
sleeping is not an emotion.

A child, I rubbed my eyes to see
the dance and tumble of colored particles

then tried to see
only blue or green, one color only

and staring into that dance fell off and often
woke in a fall, no idea where I was.

It was another life.
Sometimes I leave

my body as I sleep
drift through misted scenes

years, clouds gauzed across a sky.
Puffy, bulky clouds. Brumey, spiritous clouds.

6.

I have waited for visions
of the Virgin in holy fogs
Jesus on a cloud—
scenes painters love to paint.
I stand within the netting of a bridge
mist rising from the water like a steamy soup.

I cannot see where the world stops
and the self begins.

I shudder and fumble as a sperm must
the moment it knows
it will headlong into an egg,
the thin membrane forming around it.

I wonder was I conceived in fog,
in sorrow, boredom, fear.
A girl who made a body of a lazy eye.
Something is changing in what I call familiar.
Once what I knew best
my mother's face, would split

apart, become strange
the harder I looked.
It sneered, the eyes ran
into the ears, the mouth, the hair dissolved.
I could make her disintegrate
bring her back with a squint.

7.

Malocchio. The Evil Eye.
Horns out. *If there's a mote* . . .
Something wicked in that dark
inner half of the right,
the floating flecks in the other.
I stared and stared.

I rubbed steam from the bathroom mirror
to uncover my face and shoulders.
In my parent's room I stood on the bed
to see my breasts and hips and legs.

I arranged the pieces.
I assembled myself.

This dull sleep makes my skin buzz,
makes me dream favorite dreams—
water, water, waves, I break
things down to their familiar states:
solids to liquids, liquids to gas.
I condense, I evaporate.

8.

Mornings I relive my childhood
as I place first the right, then the left
lens in my eyes.
My face becomes whole before me,
flat, framed in the glass.
Each part sharpens, comes into focus.
(This is the most difficult moment.)

I lift myself from dreams
that lapse or joint, that crack in the fabric.
Beneath my skin the map of veins
you see in a hand above a candle,
when the flame illumines blue patterns
through skin thin as a fetal sac,
reveals the work beneath.

I can see through myself.
I see through every part of me—
I am all eye.
My body blinks,

bends the light that strikes it.
A lens for a life
buried in these eyes

the long roots grown down,
washed in their salt.
Histories of amnesias
visual, sexual, rain
through my eyes. I am light
as a saint, radiant
waves pass through me.

Integrity is wild
and many parted.
One eye joins
the other
steady, steadily
beams out
onto the world.

Buildings fall
and missiles obliterate cities.
Billboards, churches, crumble and merge
their letters and bells
scatter and rejoin.
The light hurts,
but clarity has its own beauty.

At the Exhibit of Peter Hujar's Photographs, Grey Art Gallery, NYC, 1990
for Michael Maggiar (1951–1993)

I see my face reflected in the glass, thrown back
at me as I weep for the dead and fear
for the dying. I conjure the images of friends
as though I could divine which will be struck,
the way a douser holds a stick that begins to start
and shake when water is near.
I want to hide my friends from God.

I barter with God for the lives I would save,
offer up what I want to keep what I love.
Let me be lonely, ugly, blind. Let me live
to know terrible defeat.
Catholic, I understand this magic.
Candles crossed at the neck,
statues and trees that bleed at Easter.

Inside the frame a man looks out
from his hospital veil. I see my friend's wild stare
as I saw him last night, as I stretched him out
candle wicks flickering, wavering flames
sending a gold glow to the ceiling
from under the amber globes.
Sage burned the air around us. Herbs for healing.

He condensed as I worked the hard muscular body
pressing to release him, feeling past him

to *it*, hoping it entered in pleasure
this man who would never refuse. Was his body
already yielding in photographs ten years ago?
How ridiculous now our plane ride, changed plans
how—yes—how miraculous

really, the missed train, broken suitcase,
the way our bodies are taken
by the shape of a torso, by desire.
I slid my hands up his familiar, unquiet spine.
Is a virus just another mystery inside,
like the soul, or the way a dream seems
as though we've dreamed it before?

Frame after frame, eyes stare out of beautiful bodies
in an innocent time, yielding,
eager for the moment.
I stare back at them, at my own reflections,
and imagine the photographer, himself now dead,
standing above the metal sink, developing
these faces as he presses the blank

sheets down with a stick, dousing
the paper, conjuring lives as images
rise, spread across the white sheets erasing
the blank. And I think of the superstitious who refuse
to be photographed. How we laugh at them,
they who would shield themselves
from our reflections.

Girl, Gingerpot, Tree

At twenty I willed the eggs to stop
falling through their long tubes.
I could not bear their heavy descent,
the thickness of my blood, the weight
of a man twisting and sweating above me.
I could not bear the changes in his face
the knotty bone of sleep pressed against the wall.

I dream bent men, earth grubbers,
falling into graves
or climbing out of them.
Night is a skin
tough and coarse, porous as citrus peel.
The postcards taped to the walls—
girl, gingerpot, tree—
move freely between worlds.

There is a shudder between my father and myself.
What I don't know is formless, unsayable:
the stiff fur bristling,
the ghost-green dayshirt hung
between the kitchen and the living
room, through the vibrous nights
under the silent clock

while he slept upstairs in an uneasy bed.
Father of untouched promise.
Mother of despair.

Their knotted sleep, habitual as breath.
I took from him an agony of words,
my flat eyes,
my fear of silence.

What I've learned, I've learned
fingertips to eyelids,
night wind at my backbone
unremembered song thickening my tongue,
gut-slung in the soft sexual mud
the bloods of my ancestors
healing my ancient heart.

At thirty the eggs begin again
to crawl their dazed descent.
Slow, distracted, as things go
when there is only one direction.
A leisurely fall: steady, somnambulistic.
I am the grave of many stars
this travel embedded in me.

Today for the First Time I Listen

to the hum of my body turning
itself into a nest you have pressed into
ready to begin that long forming—
liquid, hungry, blue as breath.

Coiled thing, little dividing wheel, I read
your name in the spidery glyphs the grass
leaves on my thigh.
I am not prepared for you.

Already now I feel you
siphoning my calcium and time,
racing, cleaving, as I lie here remembering my own
eager lean into being.

You make me strange to myself, turn
my urine bright. I am tidal, tender.
I listen to you through rock-picking days,
backyard winters

when I was young enough to think the sun
a yolk. Maybe you are older than I am.
Did I form you as a child
deciphers clouds, peoples the skies?

My own mother did not plan for me though I'm told
I was not unwanted.

She made a place for me.
There was not enough air for the two of us.

Our battles were ancient,
weighted,
she refusing to yield
what she'd already given up.

What piece of me did you take to spin
the membrane you drew about yourself?
Wretched invader, barely larger than thought,
I am sorry for you.

You might be the fear that rocked my grandmother,
held my mother
flat to the grain of a damp wall,
years of darkness, a mineral inheritance.

I could pluck you out
the way I slide a blade of grass
easily from the earth,
the green giving

to a white shaft where the root would be.
Or I could listen to you take me,
the way disease takes a tree, quietly,
weaving a dense and sticky cloud through its boughs.

Getting Out of Where We Came From

I was born in Brooklyn.
Even the birds were dingy
and the dark courtyard between
buildings filled with grimy light
like the lit up inside of a pumpkin.
There we could be frantic.
There we could stamp and spin
or fall down pretending to be dead.
It is still the place my father loves.
I see him: slicing meats,
stampeding streets in wild teenage goodboy crowds,
so near to me, on the lip of my dream
green workclothes still oil the air
of my bedroom, saturate the walls.
He works hard for you seven days a week.
In 1963 grease-soaked, shadowed, we ferried the harbor
to a new duplex. The model home.
Barbecues, mortgages. *Where will we get the money?*
The bridge went up. The basement flooded.
Up to our knees in water we bailed and bailed.
In their yards the neighbors laughed
and drank and shook their heads, *Too bad
they didn't know the house was built on swamp.*

Learning to Swim

Breathing in, breathing out
the cylinder of my body filling with air,
I begin to feel the architecture of myself, the internal
    scaffolding,
the weight and shape of my organs, the fish hanging inside,
myself moving through space, cutting away air,
a tear in the membrane, as when a friend dies,
the hole in the place where that life should be,
a long rip in the world.

I abandon myself to the horizontal,
the push off, release of my feet demands the belly's act of faith:
that the water might hold me.
I hang there buoyant
the way I first straddled a man's hips,
clenching and letting go
that I might go on falling,
the long hollow of my body afloat, beyond sex, beyond
the rituals of parking lots, beyond pornography and holding,
spreading wider, filling with the salt and liquid of another,
inviting the strange, invasive bacteria.
The weather of another meeting the weather of myself.
How to go on living with all this strange bacteria floating
    inside me.

By the pool's edge a woman's arms arc beneath my torso,
fall without ending,
a long, uninhabited place,

pieces of voices between here and the other side.
I contain fish and tadpole, monkey and squid, the amoeba, the
    sea anemone unfolding inside me.
A woman scaly, long, and green.

How can I give up the safety of walls, vertical certainties,
chairs, bridges, the taste of fear?
We die every day, leave rooms, bodies behind,
wander between giving and holding
remembering the groping in movie theaters,
clumsy fingers at zippers and hooks,
leave our rooms, bodies, minds billions of times over.
How do I swim in this heart and not drown?

Trusting the molecular movement, I drift out
over the failures of mothers, closets of childhood, over the
    sooted windows of Manhattan,
inquisitive fingers, kissed mirrors of bathrooms,
through the folds of my body (and no place untouched by
    water).

I fear nothing:
        nothing beneath me in the slap of the water
        nothing left of me in the tumble of sex
        nothing there of me suspended in sleep

I am a battlefield, a boiler, a bridge
joining and breaking.
A woman lies in my bathtub, supple, luxurient.
She takes me inside her,
a long string of pearls dangles from the windowbars.
I rub oil into her shoulders, the green hanging about her,

the grandfather, window-eyed with swollen legs, already
    drifting past us, half in another room,
the long hall of death the Tibetans say we enter, spinning past
    grocery stores, altars, schoolyards.
As if we could cheat gravity.

How can I float with the weight of these lives inside me?

Lost, unanchored, the memory of fish too far back in me,
I am afraid what they say is not true:
that the body does not naturally float
that boats will begin sinking, fish drown
I come to nothing
look down on my corpse stretched across a muslin bedsheet.

I examine the splash and forward of bodies moving,
so many bodies and none of them sinking
each containing the deaths of mothers, distracted fathers,
floating out over the fear of the sex act, fear of embrace,
headlines, train tables. The gloved hand at the control board.

The decision to go forward, to swim, fly, to give way—
the whale floats, and the ship, and the corpulent woman who
    swims with lacy undulations
her black body arcing like a seal
the baby floating in the sac of the mother
the moonwalker.

My Mother Makes Me a Geisha Girl

It is Halloween. 1962. Brooklyn.
It is late October. Afternoon light
seeps through venetian blinds.
I am eight years old. My mother is
making me up. My mother is making me
a geisha girl, rubbing white paint
across my face, my ears, down my throat.
Under her hands, my head
tilts. She works me over, licks
the tip of the Maybelline liner, marks
a black arch across my brow, adding
the years, filling in what she knows
should be there, the exotic
curve of the eye, hooking
toward the hairline, mole dot below
the lower lip. With a slim brush
she traces red into my lips, experience
paints in the sex. Blue shadows. Green shadows.
One hand twisting the hair from the nape
of my neck, she grips the bobby pins
in her mouth, talks through the narrow slit
in her teeth. *Hold still*, she says,
and *blot* and *blink*.
She lightens, darkens, leaves
a pile of my mouths on crumpled Kleenex.
She is back

       in 1947. Coney Island. A ride
called the Caterpillar, strapped by her date

in her seat. The lights go down, the puckered
larva begins to close, the boy
wraps his arm around her; she has waited
for this moment all her life: lipstick fresh,
stocking seams straight, her stomach flutters, she
stiffens, feels the vomit rising, she smiles
sinking, thinking *this is not right*, the Caterpillar
crawls through the tunnel, worms in the dark,
vomit rising, she backing away. This she tells me
as if to say *the body knows*. My body

does not know how to move in this pink
satin kimono she wraps about me. I choke
in the sweet cloud of her
Evening in Paris she sprays through my hair,
daubs at my throat. The body knows.
What my mother knows works on her, working on me.
Mincing steps, intricate hipwork. I can't
roll like the curve of my mother. She belts
me in, making a waist where no waist is.
My mother shows me how to be sexy. Shows
me my face in the oval mirror. I look

like a doll, all powder and posing,
wanting my own eyes back. How many faces I am.
I hunker down into a small knot,
a dark place where faces float
belly up like bloated fish. The girl
in the mirror is crying, her mother yelling
white paint smearing steamy shadows rolling
down mixing red blue black green.

City Lives

At the slope of the bridge ramp, the damp air
alerts me: the shadow shapes of dismantled
fire escapes that cling to gutted
buildings like the ghosts

of families that moved in and out over
its hundred and fifty years. The steaming soups,
unlatched trunks, the blankets and clutching. Inside,
the figures of men

balance on ladders, drop beams to the concrete
floor, hoard the unformed metals of desire,
building for future shadows. Tired their own
lives, hammer and wrench

strapped to their belts. They climb down, drink coffee from
steaming cups. The city rises in circles,
an iron garden. Lives weary from continual
transplant growing thin,

bloodless. What grows here? Not money, not time, not love
in the mother who stuffs cakes in her son's mouth
then drags him to school; not love in the newsstands
their scandals and deaths,

the naked bodies glossy, crude in the morning air,
where a girl chews a bagel she found in the

trash. Three boys circle bicycles across the
access platform, over

the FUCK WANDA metal plate where weeds push through
concrete. Where the ramp arcs I lean over the
railing, stare into my own windows. I am
naked inside there

watering a line of spiky plants, watching
a crowd of Chinese women press to the door
of the live poultry store, waiting for their fresh-killed
chickens while a man

in a bloody apron takes each one with a
lift, twist, hack. Through the curtain I watch how I
moved there, unpacked, broke a wineglass, how a voice,
a leather jacket, hand-

gun followed me up the stairs, how I walked the
rooms without sleeping, bit a seashell before
the mirror at midnight. Teeth without kindness.
Took a husband in-

to those rooms, wore warpaint into the marriage
bed, hung the walls with blue masks, maps of cities,
waiting for my face and nakedness to meet.
I leave myself there,

standing in the doorway, rubbing the mezuzahs
of old tenants, clefts thick with layers of paint.
Morning ghosts the city in fog and exhaust,
the steams from open

manholes—runic scrawls on their metal tops
warn of dangers underground, the steams of lusts
and rages seeping out. What lives in the buried
echoes of this earth?

The river, a gray bowl indistinguishable
from sky, air, bridge, as the striations and cracks
trapped inside ice. Manhattan stands in pieces:
steeples, bridge-tops, buildings,

domes, billboards, clocks, watertanks. Fragments like
nonlocking jigsaw parts. Haphazard the centuries
hang side by side, each person a seam where two
beings beat together,

birthed, deposited their urgent minerals.
The brick and blood of the city fuses them,
builds a story of the mismatched parts, binds one
life to another.

Claim

Finally I just go down to bossa nova by the river
my father in my legs and all the city breathing.
The silver arm of the Williamsburg Bridge links me to
     Brooklyn. My beginnings.
I pushed through the groins of dancing people who dipped and
     spun
groaned under each other. The dim lights over the hi-fi,
the language of belly and bone,
a child spasmodically rocking a crib across the floor
one wall to the other,
the crucifix, the tilted landscapes,
black slip on the doorknob *cha cha cha*.
Where failure was as easy to catch as measles I filled pages with
     the letter *I*—
the long bar linking sky and earth.
I dreamed prairies, decimals, blue horses, universities.
Over the tailfins of a black '58 Chrysler riding over the BQE
I saw a neon BRUNO hanging in the sky.
My father's name—spread beneath the moon, across the sky.
By the knees of the bridge the river spins and stirs.
I broke loose, headed east to glitter and coast,
attached myself to this, to that,
                     and end up at the river
grapevining the sidewalk, following the crossed bars,
leading the city with my hip,
smokestacks like trumpet valves
playing the boundary between failure and grace.

IV.

Early Morning Window

The sun begins at the river rising up
above the wet street,
over the London planes, their tough leaves starting.
It spreads across my morning table,
light in the dark cooling tea.
Today my life is precious to me.
This specific life. What I have pulled out. Attended.
Years, days, built like a ladder of sheets
tied end to end, thrown over a window ledge
down to streets where I followed a starved woman
carved with a hunger that muscled into me.
Hunger I fed on.
Where I stood naked, dazed in the afternoon traffic,
the moon-struck blood backed up in me,
coating my bones. Red, the first sign of healing.
Where a song, a voice, a woman taught me the way
to eat bread, translate the tangled blue-red lines of maps.
Days as grass. Flesh as grass.

An old woman carts her life back toward the river.
What visions have toughened the skin on her stiff hands?
I see past her withering flesh to the bright egg inside her.
Her body the diminishing placenta.
Three boys run past, test the bounce in their new sneakers,
        spring
sounds steadily across the playground's voices.
An old sound. Only the faces change

as the city continues itself. Each day
leaving something behind.

Across the street a truck lurches. Its exhaust
reminds me of my father. One night
I climbed out his window clutching
a birth certificate, a tooth, a lock of hair,
a family photo snapped at an ocean boardwalk,
a telescope tucked under my left arm.
A green girl-shaped thing dragged after me,
I dragged after her. Her form
shifted with sea-dreams,
gargoyles with leering lips,
the dull toll of words.
As I lay in the shade of her light I traced
a man's eyes ringed with too many years,
work that never fed him.
Hazel eyes, the color of fear.

How many years before a girl becomes a tree,
the seen and unseen exchanging places?
How did I escape to this life, to learn to love
this breeze that blows up the wide
street from the river?
If I close my eyes the sun in my face
remembers shirts, sheets flung across bushes,
my grandfather's hands dusted with flour and prayer,
photographs that began in a moment
and in time became history.
It's an old tale: surpassing the family,
feet pressed against the road out of there

like a cemetery of angels reaching their marble arms
at odd angles toward the sky.

Go into your own ground and learn to know yourself,
whispered a light-filled man in the dark
ages. Centuries later an old cobbler found his life
gazing into a pewter dish.
They are here now, where tongues of fire
descend over each car hood,
where the green shape wavers still
my body learns to float
to drift in the light of the cooling tea
while day bells tongue their soft chimes
through the air, through this dense life,
rolling, unrolling.

Scared Hearts and Tar

They say I dreamt it,
the tunnel behind the oak chest,
a passage though the building
out to the street.

Nanna. The oak chest. Hermits in the cookie tin.
I tell my sister the raisins are waterbugs
then crush them to show her: farm mud, the spicy dark
Italian fall, terra cotta statues

on a ship from Italy to Brooklyn.
Guarda piccolina. Che cosa fai?
Chestnut smells deep by the doorlight
to the cellar, the padlocked bins

mice and spiders and washing machines
the wet smells of drying sheets.
In the back, behind black bars
the boiler thrums like an iron heart.

I grab my sister, run to the courtyard
caught between buildings. Clotheslines
crisscross up the four stories,
Rose Velotta reeling in her husband's shirts.

The rusted pulleys shriek, resist, and the clothes
look dirtier after they're washed.
Upstairs Michael Pergola's trains loop all day
around a braided rug—nowhere to go—

as Mrs. Pergola slides another angel-
food cake into the oven. *Walk softly, lightly.*
There I bit a glass ornament, the tiny silver
manger scene shattered and Jesus in pieces in my mouth.

The sky pressed down across the building tops
like a giant Tupperware lid, sealing
the cooking steams that rose up kitchen walls:
spaghetti, cabbage greens, the thickening pies.

We counted twelve windows up the side of each brick wall.
Forty-eight windows, the sill soot like smeared mascara.
But mostly we followed the ground, trapped
ants in paper cups, covered them with holy cards.

Grandpa's cards. The scared heart of Jesus pointing
to the arrows, bars across his heart.
I am the way, Jesus said.
Suffer little children.

Blotches of tar, scars across concrete.
Grandpa wandered from crevice to crack,
stooped over holes. With a pail of hot tar
and a flat doctor's stick, he filled and scraped.

When he left we dug it out.
With spoons and sticks, rocks, toothpicks,
and broken toys, we tore, we scraped,
we ripped out the tar.

Elements of Passion

Once when I thought of passion, I imagined the flames
licking, tonguing the robes of St. Joan,
her face tilted, eyes reflecting fire.
She knew fire, the way voices burn inside,
lead a woman out. I envied her that.

A child, I watched her burn at the edges
of the TV screen. Her phosphor
glowed in the room when I turned the TV off.
It was then I dedicated my life to those voices
though it would be years before I realized it

was my mother's voice
fanning a low flame until the wind
caught it. Lifted it.
It peaked when I peaked.
I was waving with it,

carried it into my bedroom.
The mattress sagged. The blood came
into my face as I leaned into the sticky green
iridescent bedspread. I locked my sister out, rocked
into the wall, the honeysuckle, muscular oak.

There was a fireman next door. The hairs moved
over his thick arms as he laughed. He watched me
undress before the kitchen window

where the Purple Passion leaves my mother pinched each day
leaned toward the sun through the curtains.

Things burned in that room.
The curtains burst into flame,
my father's bathrobe smoked, the flank
steak my mother snatched when the oven erupted.
I ran for water. My mother screamed *salt!*

her voice raged as I hurled the crystals
through the air and over her,
as she dropped the steak and our lives returned to normal.
Now I think passion is not the fire, not the burning
but that hollow you feel when you ache for a touch,

that heavy vacuum that swells inside
the man who enters the ground each day,
who would have been a pilot, flown over continents,
the woman who listens to a man sleep, untouched
on the other side of a wall,

who envies that man his own touch,
the child who dreams pianos, cellos,
dreams only, the pull of sound from wood,
the firemen attacking a fire, spraying the flames
what they cannot do to their women

taunting them as they hold their hoses higher,
their desperate aim at the flames,
fire rising, wind rushing to meet it, igniting
a wooden hysteria erect inside their wives.
Whole lives suffering under that rubber.

Bewilder

When she could no longer pretend
to keep track of each crackle in the trees,
snap of branches, when even the moon
was not bright enough to help her
keep to the path, black flies buzzed
in her hair, the mosquito's one-note
hum deep in her ear, she heard
a shriek from the invisible
thicket of trees and could not know
what it was. She had never gone so far
into the woods. She felt she was becoming
someone else. Something kept her moving
farther in, although it was dark.

(Guests in a house nearby heard
something shrieking in the night.
Not all, but some awoke. One woman went
so far as to dress thinking to save
whatever it was—it might be a woman—
it sounded like a woman—attacked.
In the morning they spoke of it,
through several days, brought it up.
It might have been an owl attacking
a groundhog, a fox slaughtering a mole.
Each had a story though none
could shake it or the sound of that shrieking
which continued for some time.)

It was like singing, once she got beyond
the fear. She slowed down, listened, thought
it was a woman's voice she heard inside
the wood. If only she could see
her hand, a glint of starlight on her fingernail,
some piece of herself. She was becoming
invisible. Everything contrived to prohibit
and entice, the branches, the wind, the continual crack
of sound through the trees, chatter of animals.
She no longer knew the brush or touch
of an insect or tree from what buzzed inside
her head, and she rested uneasily in the minds
of the guests in the house at the edge
of the wood who could not forget her,
did not wish to imagine her, preferred to think her
a mole or squirrel, some fur-covered thing,
who never knew what happened, who rarely themselves
took walks in the woods, and never at night.

Moving In and Moving Up

1.

At first they stood outside, five men and a dog.
Occasionally someone peed in the hallway.
When the cold hit they moved in, broke
the light, the lock, seven mailboxes,
spread an old yellow blanket over the grease-
tracked floor, half a doorknob, flannel shirt,
pile of shit, two empty bottles of Nighttrain,
and a plate of dried *frijoles*.
And now I see it's my old yellow blanket.
There's a cup of wine in my mailbox slot,
three white rocks, several pennies,
and a pink plastic Happy Dolly Dream
House tipped against the wall.
By Christmas two make it to the first landing.
The dog looks dead. The man deader.
They've yelled *Ivanhoe* through my dreams.
I hear them starving in my nights.

2.

The world is structured on its own displacement,
I read in the *Times*. I think of this as I step
across the yellow blanket. Something moves,
grabs my leg. I kick it, feel for my keys.
"If I lost my keys I'd kill myself," a voice
behind me says. "Why don't you," I say.

His tongue dangles, drips on his shirt.
"I love you," he says. "God bless you, mommy."
"Fuck off," I say, hooking the keys around my finger.
"How come you so pretty? How wide you spread
those pretty legs, mama, white girl, tight pussy?"
"Merry Christmas, mommy," the blanket shouts.
"Drop dead," I say, taking the stairs two at a time.

3.

I flip open the *New York Times Cookbook*
like it's the *Modern Witches' I Ching*. P. 175:
Wash tongue and place in large kettle.
Cover tightly and bring to boil.
Simmer until tongue is fork tender.
Let cool in broth. When cool
remove. Cut off bones
and gristle at the end. Slit the skin
from the thick end to the top.
Return tongue to broth to reheat—
or serve cold.

4.

The coldest night of the year.
The one called Angelo falls down
Delancey Street, a plate of *habichuelas* in his hand,
pants around his knees, penis like an old balloon.
In the hall a man stumbles, tucks
another inside his blanket,

covers him with a cardboard box top,
wedges a clump of foam under his head,
pats it three times before he falls.

5.

Night life. He rises above me, rooting
in the caves of me. The Williamsburg Bridge
a halo behind him. I watch my legs flying in the shadows
the bridge lights strike against the wall.
That's when I feel them
climbing through the halls
moving slowly up the stairs
hand over hand, to the
second landing. *I love you,*
baby, love you, mama.
I hear them wheezing in my room,
crawling in my air,
slowly, slowly
nesting in my bed.

Diorama

Mostly I loved the glue—the sexual
smell of it, the ways it held
things together: little paper people
clipped from magazines, stiffened
with toothpicks crossed at their backs
propped on the ground like Jesus and the Thieves,
grass tufts sprung from the dirt, houses, trees,
a cardboard bus dumping its passengers
onto the street. Who knew this town?
Nothing made it particularly anywhere,
the occasion signifying more than the place,
the crude backdrop glued, smoothed, buckles
and wrinkles pressed flat.
I loved the word *perspective*, how I learned
to draw a horizon line at the back,
its black hump supporting a church
the size of a person.
And I loved the way my mother moved
around the room offering me pieces
of the kitchen life: toothpicks, coffee lids,
Saran Wrap to let the light through. She held
the plastic tight as I glued each edge
to the shoebox. Tight but not so tight it left
stretch marks across the open front. With a slight
synthetic shimmer it revealed
its scene like the floating embryo
on the cover of *Life* sealed and orbiting
in its amniotic room. I loved the way life held

in there: fixed, nonspecific. No one
died. No love was taken back. Even
when it was old, forgotten, upended
under my father's workbench. When maybe a person
had broken loose, rattled in the airtight box,
released.

Bridges

1.

One lane open on the pedestrian walkway
we weave our bikes through walkers,
baby carriages, wheelchairs, on this first
sleeveless morning, heading out of the city.
The Verazzano south, the Manhattan, the Williamsburg, north.
Cable and caisson. Tower and beam.
Steel arches stretch across the river.

Under Construction the sign flashes warning.
Around a bend the path narrows, fenced
in net. A webbed mesh stretched
overhead. Below us, over the car lanes
streetlight necks bend under their veils.
A row of nuns at prayer.
The bridge is breaking, the cables rotting.
Suspended, we weave, pedal
across the East River, past the Watchtower
into Brooklyn.

2.

It's a straight line across Ocean Parkway,
the bike lane clear.
Brooklyn. Transistor radios and baseball cards,
the sweet and easy boredom
of traffic, bagels, Anchor fences,

waiting for our blackened fathers.
Brooklyn. No books. No dreams.
"Do you think we'll have a child?" he asks.
On either side the buildings razed, rebuilt
newer, higher, *1-2-3 Bedroom Condos*.
We pedal fast, the wind against us
puffing out our shirts.
There is nothing to tie us. We could do anything.
Head anywhere. "I don't know," I say,
"Do you think there is a child waiting in us?"

Church Avenue. Avenue I. Avenue U. We pass
Avenue X, cross Neptune
to Brighton Beach.

3.

We chain our bikes to the boardwalk rail,
watch steel cranes painted
red, yellow, blue, bright as toys,
reach above the buildings.
The Tony G. Pellegrini Construction Company
squeezing another building at the lip of the shore.
Facing the ocean rows of blocky Russian headlines.
"More and more people moving out here," a voice under a
      flapping rag complains.
"They're pushing us to the ocean. Pretty soon we are
where we came from." Remnants, I think, watching
the rags and plastic tacked across windows
of the half-built building billowing
out, forced by the wind, but holding on.
Holding on.

Behind them the wheels and steeples of Coney Island—
iron rails, Astroland, and the Cyclone spiraling its steel head
    into the clouds.

We lean across the rail, face the Atlantic, dare
to look out into this emptiest
ocean, emptiest sky, while a young child
places one foot, slowly, then
the other, walking an invisible tightrope
this miniature human engine swings out,
spins one cartwheel, then another,
across the sand, to the water.

Prayer

I waited for Jesus beneath the groin vaults of Holy Cross,
Sunday sermons bellowing up, echoing down
old women weeping, *Tantum Ergo Sacramentum*
the listless hiss of lips over rosaries
kneelers knocking, bells ringing,
and the damned screaming *please, oh please*.
Pray, sister whispered, clicking down the aisle
as traffic jammed and flashed on Church Avenue.

I waited for Jesus over a counter of cards:
long, brown-curled Jesus, gentle girl-faced Jesus
naked Jesus, towel around his loins
before the rock Jesus, I am the way Jesus,
these are my hands Jesus, put your hands in my holes.
Let the one without sin Jesus, the most bloody of all Jesus,
bow your head when you say Jesus, raw meat of his heart.

I waited for Jesus by the red vein of a rock,
rolled through dust-green mountain track past
the unfamiliar splash of a brook,
birdcall and birdcall
the hideous spectacular cackle of one black hawk.
Someone said *hunger* and I tripped past fossil and stone
skidding over mossweed, slipping
through the cunt-flower of slit black ore.
Through root-knot and mud stone I rolled
through bud of hill and lip of stream I rolled
through egg-clot and deer scat I rolled

Hare Krishna Jesus
Baruch Atah Adonai Jesus
La ilaha illa 'llah.

By the headlights of a black car, the roll and dance of branches
over the twist and hip of highway, I rode a radio wave back.
My river, my city, my bridges silver in the night
rooted in pipes and wires, boilers, subways, phone lines,
rippled tin, sewer systems, all the silver twisted things beneath
    the city.
And beyond the stop signs
past the streetlights, over the rows and rows of windows
I wait for Jesus where the neon *Domino*
Sugar sign hangs
red across the river.

For My Husband Sleeping Alone

Every night now my husband falls
asleep with the lights on, bent arm
hooked around his head, book tented
across his face. His mouth is open,
lips move as though searching
(here, I imagine) for me. One cat
rests its nose to his armpit, the other,
above his head, moves with his breath.
Sometimes at two or four he wakes to shut
the light, shift, adjust the covers.

Alone in that bed he is half of something, and wholly
himself. A gentle man, a man who could fall
in love with a difficult woman. He holds
her shape beside him. Sometimes she is silent.
Sometimes she hisses and ticks.
I want to ask if he keeps
to one side of the bed—leaving space for her
as you leave unplanted soil between seeds.
Breathing room.
Does he think he will grow into her?

Myself, I sleep in the dark, opposite another
of me sleeps in the mirror. I am a couple.
Sometimes I wake, stumble across the room
blurting words I don't understand
in the morning. Words I forget. *Hunger*
is one I always remember. Each day we speak

on the phone, tell each other how we have slept.
I missed you, we say, as though we'd passed
up a chance, as though one of us were a ball
the other had not caught.

Each separation an awful rehearsal
(I know this from my own nights alone in that bed).
So I think I know why he moves into night
lights on, sheltered by fictions. Not to lie
in the dark and listen for the collapse
of a marriage, a home, a life.
It is hard to be married
and left—even for a short time.
To drift, unanchored, untouched.
To rock alone in shapeless night.

When I Understood

When I understood my mother
might have something in her
down there—she could not name the place—
growth—she could not say the word—
it is growth, after all, she fears
(how she must hate the way
her plants grow from their roots out,
pushing against the windows,
their flat heads pressing to leave)
when I understood I felt her
at the other end of the phone
(I have never called her enough)
imagined her at the table, her restless
cabinets stained behind her, her praying
hands on the refrigerator,
when I understood she had to wait,
she who cannot bear
fear, but let fear grow in her,
let fear press down through her to me,
infuse her children, bloom and tumor in them,
when I understood I did not hear
It's probably nothing, nothing being
what I fear most. I saw my mother
already slipping, she whose beauty
I have prized, worn as a badge, taken
on faith. I wanted her
whole, every part of her untouched.
I imagined for the first time her naked

body, that swollen room I formed in,
corridor leading to her heart.
It had always seemed a prison, my body
shaped so like her own, my life
trapped in hers. But now I saw her,
not as flower, not O'Keeffe blossoming
tongue and lips, flat as canvas, now I saw her
full lush red flesh. I wanted to grow back
to her, my forming body, first growth in her
red fleshy vestibule, my skin
wet with promise. I wanted
to grow back to the time I was the first
to enter, the first to come through
and what will never change
the pushing, pressing first to leave.

The Sky Could Send You

Tonight in the shadow of alien green,
the dark around us breathing,
a man points out the obvious
stars. I stand beside him under the cosmic mess.
Clutter, I whisper, you could connect anything,
join any dots to form a dipper or belt.
My eyes cannot find any cluster twice.
What I want to say is that it frightens me
this wide sky with its litter of stars.
What I want to say is you could lose yourself
in a sky like this. Looking into the flicker
of history, already dead to somewhere else.
There is so much time in a sky like this,
in our silence and the strangeness
of these ancient stars. Islands of light.
They remind me of my dead friends, my infidelities.
This night with its shadows and monsters
is too big for me. Random, irrational
as love, no matter what pictures we pretend to find.
Is this why we make a dipper or belt?
To contain it, make it familiar?
Where are the gods in a sky like this?
It is very clear, the man beside me is saying,
but I am lost. I see nothing.
Night looks like a broken thing,
as though an enormous lamp had shattered
scattering pieces of itself throughout the dark.
Is this why lovers reach to touch one another

beneath the night sky, filled with its dead stars
and fusions? Why they turn and orbit
about one another when the sky could send you
so far into yourself you would become
someone else. *The moon is beautiful,*
I read somewhere, *but dead.*
I look up into the cavey dark, the silence.
I have never understood the position of stars,
never seen either dipper, never traced Orion's
belt, seen a bull, a bear,
an arching centaur in the sky.
Patternless as measles the stars are.
Oh how I have wanted things to be clear:
love, promises, the random dark.
Beneath the curved horn of a dead moon
I think, listen to him, watch, this might be faith,
that the names name. This might be hope
or delusion, and maybe I do begin to see the beginnings
of a handle, there, just there,
where the lights are slightly brighter.